SCOTTISH NOËL

(1500's)

by

Fionn Mac Colla

FOREWORD

What was it *like*, to live in those days. A desirable ultimate End of the effort towards historical knowledge must be if possible to pass through or beyond, or, more correctly, to go forward *with* the knowledge of the facts, of the circumstances and conditions of people's lives in former times, to an apprehension of the quality of their consciousness of—or simply *in*—those conditions, what the experience meant, or what it 'tasted like,' to them as they lived it. If it were possible to re-live thc past in the company of those who were contemporary with it, that would be true historical understanding. . . .

In its original form the episode described here was conceived and written as part of a projected novel which was to have been set in the sixteenth century. The fact accounts for certain elements—notably the bulking of traitors in the scene. *It is also the only, and that an incidental reason why the episode should have been placed in the fifteen hundreds.* So far as it recalls the relations that obtained between the two neighbours, and the common attitudes of the people to them, it is typical of a range of history not far short of a millenium. Except that an attack in strength at such a season of the year would be unusual—(the attack under cover of a religious festival was characteristic)—

more or less identical circumstances, and attitudes, obtained all the way from the time, about the year 700, when the Northumbrian chronicler was designating the northern nation as 'a bestial people and of savage mind' solely because they 'despised subjection to the Saxons,' down to the period of this episode, at which time army after army came north over the Border bearing the express personal orders of the English King that no human creature of the Scots was to be left alive, of any age or either sex. Those simply were the conditions in which life had to be lived. There was always the expectation, the readiness. Generation after generation, century after century. When the beacons blazed their warning from the hilltops the men of each district armed themselves and set out at once towards the enemy. And fought him wherever they found him, the odds not considered.

FIONN MAC COLLA.

Morghann,
Barraidh.
15th August, 1958.

WHO bringeth light at midnight. Who maketh a path in darkness. Who covereth the whole earth with purity as with a garment, and men sing his praises rising in the night. Whose heart maketh a conversation of love between heart and heart, and men hasten from their doors in the name of love. Whose sweetness fills the air.

Who stills the voice of the world, making a hush where many are. Who is great that lieth in littleness, a son and fathers bow down before him. Who is innocence that breaks the heart, and renewing of hope, before whom sorrow giveth place to joy. Whose praise is a harmony soaring and lofty.

Who is holiness and the humility of those that bow the knee. Who is come, and his coming now is the expectation of all. To whom is made the offering of hearts . . .

There is a passing to the right, a flutter of vestments, a moving across to leftwards.

The small red-haired priest has mounted to the pulpit. When he uncovers his head it seems in its brightness to add one to the company of the angels under the roof and the saints standing in their niches.

And angels look from Heaven when he reads in a loud clear voice . . .

Joseph gaed up from Galilee to Bethlehem in Judea with Mary his espousit wife, and her days being accomplishit she brocht forth her first-born son and wrappit him in swaddling claiths and layit him in a manger. And the angel of the Lord appearit to shepherds watching their sheep and sayit unto them: Fear not, for behold I bring you guid tidings of great joy, that sall be to all people . . .

After the Mass a tall fair-haired priest came out of the church and casting a casual glance about noticed that already the last worshippers had passed from sight. From the left, in the direction of the market-place, came slight but clearly on the frosty air the diminishing sound of footsteps in the snow. The night was piercing clear. From the house roofs right up and over the near-full moon spread a vast luminous net spangled innumerably with swimming motes. In the tingling air one seemed to hear a distant singing.

He walked a few paces to the right where there was some garden ground, cold and deserted, with irregularities of upturned soil under thin snow, and solitary vegetable stalks, motionless, each holding up a white puffed head. Beyond, the glance passed unimpeded to southward, over rolling, rising country, till it reached low hills. In the west stood motionless snow-clouds, towering masses glittering like sparkling fleece all along their upper edge, but turning a lowering face of lead-coloured surface towards the earth. To the left above the house roofs appeared in the distance like frozen billows summits of the Pentlaw Hills.

John Erskine fellow-priest, red-haired, so familiar in compact form and energetic mien, emerged from the church and looking neither to right nor left hurried across and disappeared into the shadows of the presbytery house. The tall priest hung a moment longer looking where there was a curious effect to westward—the world, snow-white-clad, appearing insubstantial, floating, while all solidity had passed into the heavy, leaden sky.

While he was admiring this rarity he began to think he detected, whether in his ears or as if down by his feet, coming along the ground, a tiny, drumming sound. He gave attention to it, trying to pick it up. At once it was unmistakable, and was growing more distinct. Rising, it seemed to swim about him—a continuous drumming sound, regular, though seeming to contain irregularities. Rapidly it drew nearer till, though still small, it drummed on the surrounding air. It stopped, and there seemed to be some shouting—at the North Port, that could only be. When it recomenced, all at once much louder, a clinking sound within it brought sudden, completest recognition—it was the sound of horses ridden at a canter! He felt surprise. To his right not far away was a corner, and here they suddenly appeared . . . some ten, twenty, thirty mounted men scattering shattered moonlight from armour and accoutrements. Even as he looked at them with astonishment they dropped to a walk and came slowly towards him along the road, breathing out their breath in a smoking cloud around them, with frosty tinkle of bit and bridle and an increasing creaking of saddle-leather. When they came abreast he saw with more astonishment that the horses had been ridden hard. As they went slowly past—the irregular clop-clop of many hoofs muffled on the snow-covered ground—the jingling of metal and creaking of leather seemed loud. The riders moving with their uncomfortable-looking motion forwards and back in the saddles. One of the horses as it passed repeatedly shaking its bridle and giving vent to a hoarse coughing. One and another among the grim, bearded men gave him an impersonal glance above his smoking breath. A number seemed however to cast what he thought were looks of some surprise about the street and more than one as they passed glanced enquiringly up at the steeple. One turned and addressed an indistinct remark in which however the word 'bells' seemed to occur to his neighbour, and then both gave an enquiring look upward. A little farther on they bore to the right and began going down the road to the south, their noise slowly going along with them. As they went down the rather steep incline the hips of the horses were seen rising and falling alternately at each step, the tails hanging limply down.

They had scarcely gone from sight, and the sound of their going was still muffled on the air, when away to northward, from the road by which they had come, rose—still more unseasonably startling—the wail of pipes. He opened a wide look before him, wondering what on the face of the frost-bound earth could be afoot this night. But hardly had the pipes risen in volume when they died again; he imagined some interruption breaking in. Again there was a drumming on the ground, some commotion or shouting in the direction of the North Port, and he found himself looking, somewhat startled, towards the corner where the road turned towards him. On the dull ground there came a sound of galloping. He waited expectantly, held by some excitement.

A big horse shot into sight. In the brilliant moonlight his eye caught the device of the armoured man sitting on its back and he took a step backwards in amazement . . . *the Bishop*! If the Bishop noticed him standing there he gave no sign. As he came abreast he addressed the horse with a sharp exclamation and touched with his spurs and the horse went belly-to-earth over the head of the brae out of sight. Immediately the whole air was full of galloping when a large body of horsemen rounded the corner flashing and sparkling in the moon and swept past in a momentarily stupefying rumble and clatter, making full speed to overtake their leader. The tall priest, considerably perturbed, stood gaping at their point of disappearance.

A man came out of the church; a man with a square dark beard—the sacristan—and seeing him approached.

"Did I hear horse?" he asked in casual tones.

But before the priest could reply he felt his shoulder clutched convulsively.

"*God's Blude*!" the sacristan was screaming at his side; and, pointing a shaking hand to southward . . . "*the beacon*!"

Wheeling about he dashed back into the church.

On the summit of a hill away to the southward a point of fire had indeed sprung up. The tall priest was gaping at it in mute incredulity when two sounds shook about him in quick succession and the peace of the night was shattered to the stars. From the road, inside the gates, the roar of pipes went up into the air. And above his head, from the steeple of the church, rang out a thunderous . . . *boom*!

Before he knew it he was flying into the presbytery house, even as overhead the iron mile-wide echo was ringingly impacted into soaring fragments by the second . . . *boom*!

Crying . . . "John! John! John!!"

Not to be seen!

He dashed to his chamber and threw wide the door.

"Up, up, John! No time now for prayers! *The English are ower the Border*!"

"What an' yet again!" cried the other getting up, and his eyes kindling:—then with a burst of anger—"I wad better ha' been a sodjer and never a priest!"

The tall priest had been in the act of turning away. He turned back. . . "It's as a priest there's need o' ye!"

he shouted—loudly, for the bells were ringing madly and the house shaking in the clamour—"Men are deean out yonder!"

He was scarcely gone when he came back... "But put a swoord on ye!"—making hopeless gestures with his hands because of the defiant screaming now shrilling past the house, and the reverberating tramp of feet—"They'll spare ye the less for that ye are a priest!"

2

Their two figures were crawling across an expanse of elevated plain all white with snow faintly ridged by a wind that was no longer blowing. Not another figure was in sight, not a point of movement anywhere—as if man had been silently subtracted from creation. Leaving only a beacon, glowing ahead, as a sign that he had once been present. Man had gone—and the voice of man. They had not spoken for what seemed an eternity; only sat muffled and remote on their horses, their eyes deep-shadowed under their brows watchfully searching the distance. In an audible silence shone down the moon. Or it was the cold striking against cold in that vast vault that made a lonely music. The eye travelled in all directions to the utmost verge and found nothing more palpable to rest upon than blue translucent shadows lying among the hills. From this boundless emptiness of a glittering world grown feathery as an illusion, shone upon by the cold moon and multitudinous stars, amid silence frozen in immensity, there came forth a measureless indifference, like an emanation creeping chill into the soul.

John Erskine realised that he must have been nodding on the horse, for it was tall Ninian Kennedy's voice beside him that brought him to himself, and his hand touching his breast. They had left the high white moor. They were standing on a road or track, with woods around casting jetty shadows. Ninian was pointing across his breast to something lying at the road's edge. It was a wayside shrine of the rude kind that countrymen put up; to which, passing, they doff their bonnets with a murmured prayer. It had been thrown down and trampled on: there were the marks of many hoofprints all about the place.

"*English!*" said Ninian Kennedy, a quality in his voice as always having the power of making all objects sit down firmly on the solid earth.

"The English of a surety," agreed John Erskine looking round with scorn, his nostrils twitching. He put his horse in motion.

They left the road and skirted upwards through the trees. Above was the moor again, snow-covered, virgin of hoofprints, and the silence. The beacon larger and nearer, right ahead.

They came to a downward slope and a red light fell on their faces. A village was smouldering below. At the farther end, lifted up above the village on a knoll, stood a roofless church, glowing red within. They looked at each other, halted; a moment later went on with watchfulness, stepping downward through the snow.

About the church the men of the place were lying, in all attitudes, young boys among them and ancient men with grey beards pointing to the sky. In front of them mounds of English dead. The heat that throbbed from the stone church reached them where they were. Covering their mouths and noses because of the corpses roasting within they sheered away, unable to approach or linger.

Soon they were skirting the base of the hill on whose summit the beacon glowed redly. Here the surface of the track was black and muddy from the recent passage of many feet of men and horses. The south side of the hill proved to be covered with a wood of medium-sized trees growing pretty closely.

"Look yonder!" exclaimed the red-haired priest, Erskine, reining back his horse. A figure in armour had stepped out from the trees and was standing, full in the moonlight, looking in their direction. Now they could detect, too, that there were men and horses in the wood. The armoured figure came stepping towards them—a very tall man in flashing steel, a sword by his side.

"Wha are ye?" challenged John Erskine as he came near, and when the soldier in reply said something in Scottish, looked back over his shoulder at Ninian Kennedy and allowed the horse to go forward a few steps. There he sat, waiting, looking out into the cold night, the cold touching his eyeballs. He looked at his horse's ears against the snow and heard the voices behind him expanding and floating, knew Ninian Kennedy's mind as always working with great deliberateness, and was conscious of the iron man standing near, gleaming coldly, an unknown element of force inside indifferent steel.

But something he thought he heard roused him to keen attention and when Ninian Kennedy rode forward to join him—coming up this time on his right hand whereas till now he had been all along on his left—he turned on him in question . . . "Did he nocht say they are fra Menteith?"

The blue eyes beside him—looking nearly white as they had done from their outsetting by reason of the continuous passing over them of the reflections of the universal snow—turned on him and immediately passed beyond him . . . "I thocht ye understood not the Scottish, John!"

Leaving the wood of men behind them they began again going forward.

"I thocht I understood *that*!" said the small priest, and went on . . . "Come tell it, Ninian, whate'er it be! I am nocht a bairn!"

The blue eyes looked at him, with something like pity . . . "If ye maun hear it, it is e'en say: they are fra Menteith."

Here they had come to another sparse wood and for some moments angled up through it in silence.

At length . . . "Ye ken weil what is in my mind!" called out the priest with the bright hair, passing through the trees. "If they be fra Menteith we are weil to the southward o' them. How then are they here afore us?"

"They were warned afore us," the tall priest called back, steering his own course.

"How could that be?"

The wood getting more open the horses came together again. As by a mutual impulse their riders drew them to a halt, almost facing each other.

"John," said the tall fair-haired priest with a sombre look, heaviness in his voice, "ye maun ken we are but latecomers. That beacon that suld ha' warned us was never lichted . . . till it was lichted by the Menteith men themsel's whan they gat here. It may weil be the men o' other different pairts are nocht in arms this nicht for that the beacons that suld hae warned them were never lichted . . ."

The small priest narrowed his eyes and waited. The other brought himself to continue only with effort. "The Menteith men fand fower deid men by the beacon, John. Fower that had been to licht it . . . afore others cam' upon them that slew them!"

The small red-haired priest started, glanced this way and that among the trees: whispered ". . . *the traitors*!" They sat looking on each other.

A sudden sound from right ahead was like a distant, heavy crash. They raised their heads and sat listening. There came a distant sound like far-off shouting.

"Far awa yet," said the tall priest and clicking his tongue to the horse began to move forward.

At the top of the ridge a man was sitting his horse in the shadow of a clump of trees whose upper arms had been made to grow out all sideways by the steady force of winds in those uplands. He turned his head, frowning, and the moonlight showing a tall priest on a grey horse and by his left side a smaller, compact of build and red-haired, on a black, raised his hand to his steel cap and turned away again and resumed his watching.

At the moment it was like a battle on a tapestry. A vast white ground was dotted over in the distance with small black figures. No sound of conflict came. But ever and again, as though a draught had rippled the stuff faintly, movements here and there could be detected and silver points would sparkle out under the moon. From the ridge where the man-at-arms and the two priests sat in the shadow of the wind-woven branches the ground sloped gently down, to a small watercourse apparently, then gently up again to a second ridge. Halfway between the watercourse and the far line of sky, on the long snow-covered slope, a strong company of Scottish foot had stood to the encounter. They were drawn up in a tight, wide circle; its centre, plainly visible to the watchers, occupied by a motionless group that seemed to be a small company dismounted from their horses. There was something menacing and implacable in the absolute immobility of that circle: it looked animate yet unhuman, suggesting some gigantic spider squatting on the slope. In front of it at various points were long black heaps.

The grisly circle still standing in its attitude of waiting menace, among the English gathered away to the right an apparently confused movement of milling about started up. They were forming into ranks: in a very little time they had shrunk and quietened to a solid object on the snow. Followed a moment when over the entire field movement seemed arrested forever. Springing to life the black etincelating shape launched itself forward, and the suddenly thin-looking circle of spears seemed even at that distance to quiver and draw together to receive the impact. Still they were like painted figures moving on a painted field, all in a watching silence. But when the attacking cavalry had covered half the distance there came a trickling in the ears that was their heavy drumming. The mass could be seen to meet and shake against the line, while the drumming still continued. Only a moment later did it change with a sudden far-off clapping, to become a tiny clangour wavering in the ears.

But the line held firm. After a time it seemed as if the mass was not so blackly pressed against the circle's rim. Then there was no doubt of it, the horsemen were retiring. White appeared between them and the long black heap left new before the spears. They drew off slowly, halted, moved to a new position on the farther slope to southward, halted again; it looked as if they would repeat their charge. But it was the end of the action. After an apparently hesitating moment they wheeled about and rode slowly away up the slope.

The last had scarcely vanished when the ring opened, a group of men mounted on small horses passed through and appeared in the open, and spreading out fan-wise trotted nimbly after towards the distant ridge. Until they reached it the spearmen below maintained formation. Then, some signal having passed no doubt, the ring suddenly crumpled and vanished and in its place was a solid column marching away doggedly in the invaders' wake. Without warning the watching man-at-arms under the trees gave an ear-splitting whistle, answered at once faintly from where the Menteith men were waiting below.

"Forward now, John!" said the taller priest, and they started down the slope.

As they approached the place the impression of a picture faded. Its smell was crude and real: of blood and entrails of men and horses with which the trampled ground was putrid, torn flesh, and sweat and leather. The dark heaps gave forth a sound: horses groaning with a human voice, and a subdued unhuman howling and muted yelping of men. They became shapes: trunks and limbs lying inextricably, many transfixed in violent attitudes. From time to time they heaved in a convulsion, some great horse rolling in its agony, thrashing with its legs; and there would rise a fearful screaming, followed by whimpers or screaming still more fearful, or else by sudden silence as some wounded wretch had his brains kicked out or was crushed under and smothered in the bloody slush.

The Scots had not escaped scatheless either. Inside the space where the circle had stood there were figures, some reclining, others motionless on the ground. Ninian Kennedy, suppressing a grimacing shudder of nausea because of the tepid acridity exhaling from the heaps, shouted, "Have you need of a priest?" and in Teutonic, "Do ye need a priest?"

Several figures moved to look at him. One stout fellow nearby seated against the back of a dead horse, his headpiece between outspread feet, half-turned and disclosed his bearded face, the lips stretched in the semblance of a wide grin or snarl because he was grasping in his strong teeth the end of a clout that he was binding about his naked forearm, which he was holding up bent across his front. Not far beyond a dark form was kneeling on one knee, stooping over one who lay extended on his back. Just then he took the hands of the recumbent one and crossed them quietly on his breast. His hand rose white in the moonlight in the sign of the Cross.

He got up: a slim man of middle height.

"Good be with you," his voice came over in casual tones. "*I* am a priest!"

The brisk jingling party on horses of different colours riding up were the men from Menteith, their tall captain on a big black in the lead. Ninian Kennedy having made his acquaintance caused his grey horse to fall in beside him. John Erskine allowed all to pass and fell in at the rear, as he did so noticing that still another party, whom he recognised at a glance as mounted pikemen, were coming up behind, jigging forward at a fast trot.

Shortly the men behind had closed the distance. He was aware of them riding at his back. He did not look round and the whole column rode steadily on together, trotting, then walking, then trotting again, all in the silent night.

The leader of the group of mounted pikemen came up behind the small red-haired priest. Without any preliminary he began in a matter-of-fact voice speaking from behind his shoulder. . .

"I had a little daughter. Three years old. Her blue eyes were ever dancing, the golden hair dancing in ringlets round her head, her little feet so light they seemed only to brush this evil earth. Ah, man, a sweet, blithe sprite!. . . Three years she brought light among us. . When the English came she laughed and danced to see the torches flaming on their breastplates and their helmets, standing before them in her shift, that scarcely covered her little rosy buttocks. The leader of them held the point of the spear towards her, making some play with it as if it was a jest, and laughing. She even put out her hands . . . such soft, warm little hands she had! And then—would you believe this, sir?—he laughed and plunged it into her body, and still laughing, threw her down against the wall. I saw her there, not long ago. Very tiny she looked. Just a flower crumpled and thrown down beside the wall. Her ringlets in the blood. Quite still. And all so sudden, you know: I couldn't take it in. And her little arms . . . folded on her little bloodied breast . . . I was standing and looking at them . . . and all the time I could feel them tightening warm about my neck . . ."

John Erskine understood this, although, town bred, he did not speak Scottish. Had he been able he would have replied . . . that woe was the common lot under this sky, the portion of all who had the English for neighbours, but that God was ever the Judge . . . As it was, he kept his face averted, merely nodding his head. But he was struck by the shuddering break in the voice behind him and looked back across his shoulder.

The eyes under the glinting snout of the pikeman's helmet were not on him but looking far into the distance.

John Erskine shrank from the close sight of that gentle, dreamy gaze which seemed to him so much more implacable than fury.

3

They were in a wood on a short northward slope, out of sight. From time to time in the clear air sounds even reached them from the English camp which lay away behind them to southward. On their left, to westward, about a mile away, another body of English cavalry could be seen through the frosted trees debouching, in ever extending procession, from a gap in low hills. From near that gap a ravine whose steep bushclad sides ran shadowed and black across the country, came curving along the front of the wood, and near the end of it, through a sudden falling of the land, dropped away to a mere bed of a frozen burn, across which the Scots, in their position in the wood, had clear access in front to some miles of level plain. The course of the approaching English would take them past the front of the wood, on the hither side of the ravine.

In the wood the Menteith captain was speaking . . . "Now, lads, we have got ourselves into a fine scrape; the watchword is silence. 'Tis our only hope. To your posts, spearmen on the left; and pray to all your saints they do not sight us or we are nothing but dead men. Let the spearmen keep shoulder to shoulder and thrust with a will; once in the ravine they should be safe enough, for the Englishmen will scarcely dismount:

they are glutted for this night and thinking only of the good Scottish beef roasting this moment in their camp back yonder. To your posts, quickly! And remember—silence, as you hope to see your mothers! Wait for the signal!"

After that there was a stealthy noise that went on for a little, with twigs crackling and occasional small clinkings. In a succession of places patches of moonlight tilted and flattened, or leapt up and slithered to the ground again over forms moving through the trees. There were glimpses of spearmen going to the left, then no more: they appeared to have gone stooping with careful steps altogether from the scene. The wood stilled, with diminished cracklings of frozen twigs ever fewer and more furtive. Then it had stilled into apparent emptiness. Only on a close, attentive scrutiny would here and there a part of man or animal be detected, picked out by the moon or marked against the light in front, a shoulder, a part of a face, an unmoving arm or elbow—till it dawned, like a blow, that the silent wood was breathing full.

On the right the horsemen were in a flattened wedge-formation, roughly because of intervening trees. The horses, experienced in the play of war, seemed by their own instinct to merge with the shapes of light and shadow: there they remained immobile, without cough or whinny. Out in front, seen through a black lattice-work of twigs and branches, the snowy level below and beyond the ravine appeared to flicker, in alternate instants blue and glistering. It was awesome, the stillness. John Erskine in his position behind the tip of the wedge, shivered involuntarily, with cold as with impatience. Down on his left the sword in Ninian Kennedy's right hand shone blue-dark against the smoky white of the horse's shadowed side. Below, foremost in the wedge, was the Menteith captain. That was his broad shoulder clearly drawn against the white ground out beyond, and the arm to the elbow, the line of the armoured body to the waist, nothing more except the side of his helmeted head. And everything in the wood minute by minute in a rock-like tenseness, a steadied impulsion of mail-clad malice, an implacable wall waiting in the shadows to go down—as it would go down—in a death-bearing crash. And that man with the father's outraged heart, *he* was waiting there now, somewhere in the wood. Recalling the gentle, dreamy look in his eyes one felt the cold increase. As if the earth were breathing it outward from itself, in rhythmic gusts. With each in-drawn breath the landscape lifted, and in each shuddering subsidence the trees were shaken farther apart, and the men under them stood more visible. It got more open all about, and the cold swept round as if it were a wind. Would they never come?

There came a faint jingle, a quiet clopping, muffled voices heard intermittently, passing along the face of the wood. After a long time in which the sounds were continuous but appeared to come but little nearer, the farthest of the spearmen with a faint surprise saw them already passing before the tree trunks. In twos and threes, riding easily in the secure and unsuspecting sense of nearness to their camp. More and more of them moving with short irregular forward jerks on their walking horses, so many hoofs with a faint continuous hiss disturbing the snow. Their steel helmets flashed continuously, on breasts and backpieces and armoured points sparklings were incessant. Ever and again there were plumes and pennons. The displacement of their easy passing through the crystal stillness came like a chill breath among the trees and feather-light touched eyes and cheekbones. When one of them said something in his own language to his neighbour it was surprisingly distinct, and the short laugh that followed.

On they went. with their leathery creaking: it seemed miraculous that not one so far had turned to look into the wood. Now many had passed along, more and still more were coming—it seemed strange there was no signal.

The first score or so had gone airily past the point where the horsemen were in hiding when from the wood, startling at last even those within it, rang out a clear, bird-like call. Instantly the long line rippled to a halt, though at the head, opposite the place where the sound had risen, was trampling and prancing of startled horses. Farther back along the line heads wagged from side to side but in front all were turned in apprehension towards the wood, under whose cover the land seemed, by the noise, to be sliding towards them. Out from the trees leapt like an apparition a giant with levelled lance on a black horse, and after him and on either hand, at once blurring and reinforcing the impression, others amid a furious bursting of twigs. Even then, while the shocked senses strove to rebut and balance, they received a still more stunning blow, for a cry, weird and strange, rose wavering above the countryside, chilling the blood of those who heard it. The horses at the head of the column danced on the ground; their riders in consternation strove to control them and simultaneously to draw or point their weapons. But gaining impetus at every leap the attackers came like a wind, and before those weapons could be drawn or pointed, and while the echo of that grisly cry still hung in the air, there was a heavy thudding of bodies against bodies, a simultaneous clash and loud outburst of cries of anger and alarm: riders were swept out of their saddles and vanished, horses—seen backing up, pawing the air—were whirled about and bodily overborne; and after what had seemed no more than a jar or momentary checking of their headlong course the ambushers were through the line, had crossed the burn below the ravine and were away, opening out across the glittering level with diminishing four-footed sound.

In their wake some of the wreckage moved: men were raising themselves on hands or elbows in the trampled snow, some endeavouring to regain their feet; several riderless horses had gone cantering a distance after the Scots as if drawn along in the vortex of their flight, and now they were stopping one by one, looking, with heads up and ears pointed, after those they had been following, then wheeling round and trotting on the way back, but with checkings, haltings to lift their heads, and bewildered neighings. But on the ground some of the human wreckage lay quite still, with faces in the snow, or on their backs with outflung arms, in patches suddenly and swiftly grown red.

Thus so far everything had gone as hoped and planned. The score or so English at the head of the column as soon as they had apprehended the situation, and having a clear field before them, fled helter-skelter, energized doubly on the breaking out of that unnatural cry. Came the clashing impact. Those immediately in rear of it were thrown backwards or threw themselves backward upon the ranks behind, and as at the same time those farther back were pressing forward towards the point of the disturbance a confused mass was formed of horses packed together, some endeavouring to make forward, some to extricate themselves and retreat to greater safety, many held motionless in the press. The coolest might shout, *They are but a few! Follow!*—but the resulting movement such as it was only made the press closer and more effectively blocked advance.

That was the moment—the column immobilised all down its length—when the spearmen stepped quietly from the trees, and the shouting and agitation were renewed when those halted immediately behind the disordered and congested head of the column perceived themselves menaced close in on their right. This time there was nothing supernatural in the sudden fear; the spears—serpents of moonlight liquid on their venomous tips—were being borne so swiftly in by those grim close-packed men that time was lacking to wheel mounts or level lances. In a moment they had closed, and the heavy flopping attempts at turning gave place to a dancing of maddened horses when they felt the pricks. The method was to prick the horses whose rearings and plungings unsteadied if they did not quite unseat the riders, many top-heavy in full-mail. Those farthest in advance, pricked in the soft parts of their undefended rear, leapt screaming forward upon the mass now more entangled than ever because trying more desperately to disengage themselves; several were by this alone emptied from their saddles, several more while clinging on precariously, and for the moment helpless, were transfixed and brought clanging down. On the spear-men's opposite or left flank they pricked the horses in the neck or nostrils so that they reared back into and disordered the lines behind, thus holding up for a sufficient moment development of an attack. Simultaneously the same method was being used against those directly in front of the intruding spears. The horses prick-pricked at were bounding and plunging heavily, at every bound approaching nearer the ravine, while their riders rocked about could never steady to point or aim a blow and were severally either struck from their saddles or thrown out of them. Those in full armour, plume and device, came down with a clang that resounded among the excited shouting and lay still and were trampled over by the spearmen's hasty feet. Or else they were still clinging to their saddles when the frantic horses, one after the other, were driven to take to space with a final bound, and dropped, rider and all, into the darkly shadowed ravine, from which then rose the tearing and crashing noise of their descent.

The spearmen with bloodied spears were not an instant standing on the edge before vanishing into the ravine in handfuls and with precipitation. Their clambering noise could be distinctly heard passing backward along the line of the English column: a good number of their horsemen rode their horses to the edge and peered over, inclining themselves forward or sideways. There was a moment of looking about and indecision. But when one horse with a wild scream reared back with blood pouring from its nostrils the movement back was general.

Away over the snow, the party of mounted Menteith men and others were grown small in the distance.

There had been a casualty. The Scot who had been at the extreme right of the wedge of horsemen, being last out of the wood, owing to the prompt flight of the foremost files of English found no one before his weapon. The nearest, however, were still near enough for him to see the shining horse-shoes of the hindmost upturned in rapid alternation. Swerving away to his right he set off alone in pursuit. The first he overtook, a man-at-arms galloping all unsuspicious, and taking aim with his lance planted it in his back. The man rose forward off his saddle. First the reins, then his lance dropped from his hands. As his attacker came abreast and swept past he doubled over forward then in a single ponderous but rapidly accelerating movement dived heavily down past the horse's neck. When there came his dry clatter striking the earth the man ahead looked over his shoulder and saw the solitary enemy coming up on his right side, in the act of setting his lance at him transversely over his horse. He gave a startled exclamation and attempted to strike a blow backwards. The hostile point in consequence lodged under his arm and with a screaming cry he dropped his lance and fell forward on his horse's neck. A number of the score or so in front turned their heads, and at that the pursuing man made his horse swerve about and set off to overtake his party.

He had jumped the frozen burn and was stretching out at an accelerating speed across the level when misfortune in a common form overtook him. His horse set its foot in some hole under the snow and came down with such force that he was catapulted into the air. His lance soared and turned above him and landed and stood quivering in the earth after and beyond him. Three, four of those he had been pursuing seeing his plight at once wheeled and made towards him. He was attempting to get to his knees when the first came up and rode him down. Similarly the remaining three one after the other without checking speed rode him into the earth. They checked then, wheeled round and returned. The first to reach him halted, looked down, then bending forward in his saddle planted his lance-point with deliberation, withdrew it, and with the same deliberation pressed it home again. The other three coming up, all four sat their horses looking down.

The next moment the four of them were looking up, lances erect, heads turned in the direction of the wood and the halted column shining in arms along its front, atop the darkness of the ravine. Shouting had broken out there, an alarmed shouting that was getting louder. And some peculiar movements appeared to be going on in the section of the column behind the entangled mass at its head—violent movements, as if the horses were all jumping up and down together. And the shouting seemed to be centred there. When it was clear that saddles were emptying the four moved off, obliquely, keeping their heads turned in the direction of the disturbance as they moved. The shouting and the dancing up and down of horses in the column grew more and more pronounced. At length some—actually with riders on their backs—were seen to take leave of solid ground altogether and vanish down the dark slope into the ravine. At once the four broke into a hand gallop after their companions in the direction of their camp.

The fallen horse had never moved where it lay bulky in the snow. The lance some distance away stood rigid at the end of its shadow. A dark patch had grown large around the inert form between. At that moment the man himself was standing in the presence of his Maker, bearing in his hands the merit of his life given freely for a pure good of others, unconsideringly given that the spiritual flower of freedom might adorn his race in the generations to come.

No one had observed his fate. Away in the distance his party slowed and halted, turned to look back, the horses with heaving flanks breathing out their breath like smoke into the frosty air. The long line of English were seen in motion along the front of the wood, then cantering briskly towards their camp and passing out of sight.

"Quite right, my lads," the Menteith captain apostrophised them softly. "Roast beef is more comforting in the belly than cold steel. We knew *you*!"

Shortly then groups of active dots—the spearmen—began to be perceived emerging from the head of the ravine and making for the gap to northwards.

"Sweetly!" said the captain softly, sitting easily with hands crossed above the reins before him.

4

Later in the night they were back near the scene of the ambush. A group that included the Menteith captain and the tall fair-haired priest were standing by the side of the track recently hoof-beaten by the English, which not far away behind them turned sharply south towards the English camp. The moon was far down in the west. Near them, the ravine loomed jetty black: elsewhere too, shadows were growing all about. The air entering the nostrils was colder than ever. With the hour and the cold a deeper quiet seemed to have descended—seemed rather to be descending. A quiet intense to solidness. One could imagine, looking upwards, boat-shaped concavities of blueness or great translucent petals falling slowly in succession down the outer blue. In such a quiet the men moved under the stars, each animating his striding shadow on the lighted levels.

Those busy in the foreground were carrying stones in their hands or on their shoulders to the nearby spot where they were building a cairn above the man who had been killed. Fifty or sixty yards to northwards crouching or reclining figures were black against the glow of picket fires. Some two miles farther north a diffused glow hung above the position of the Scottish army. The small red-haired priest had gone there to find and remain with the men of the burgh.

"Yes, 'tis a weakness in us, Reverence"—the Menteith captain was speaking of the dead man—"I have seen a-many such happenings, and actions spoiled and even lost through it. Yes, I would say that the valiant Scottish men of our nation are altogether too headlong. Because there is a flame of manhood in them they fear no advantage in Saxon bodies, and forget there may be odds even in that commodity past what is human. Also they think so well of themselves as men of their weapons—in the which, *par Dieu*, they have reason, for there are no better in the world—that through contempt of enemies they can be worsted at times by those that fight better by the ruse and stratagem."

The tall priest was looking about, idly, in the lighted and shadowed world. "Have you thought nevertheless that the fault may come in part from this, that we Scots have always fought only in a just cause, have never tried to enslave or despoil others, only to defend ourselves. When your cause is just your eye is single, your heart pure, guile and cunning do not attract you: the issue is so clear, you think only of striking a blow for the right, and that as soon as may be. But this puts you at a disadvantage when you have to do with men whose intentions are not honourable, as English intentions towards Scotland have always been dishonourable. For by the very fact that you intend evil towards a man you will be unconsciously disposed to adopt trick and stratagem, rather than meet him face to face whom you intend to wrong. It's a sort of shame of the shameless. If you would strike a man down without cause you would as soon do it from behind; but if in a just cause you would sooner have him before you face to face. That is because the act is purified by the heart's intentions, and conduct without blame follows the desire of righteousness. Whereas evil deeds come with an evil will."

Though the silence was heavy, muting sounds near at hand, yet it could be noticed after a time that it had itself a vague background of noises in the night —far-away noises of uncertain origin that started up and were never completed, dying away with their distant echoes. The tall priest went on . . .

"That would explain the exceedingly fierce hatred the English have for us Scots, who, when all is said, never wronged them or wished to wrong them. The evil Will darkens the soul with malice towards the person wronged in deed or in intention. So it is that while there is a hatred natural in the one wronged against him who has wronged him, even a great hatred where great wrongs have been done, nonetheless the most violent hatred of all is that borne towards the innocent by him that has wronged him or purposes to wrong him. So strange a thing it is, man's heart."

"Strange and ugly if so, Reverence," said the captain. "Certain it is the intentions of the English towards us have always been black indeed, as black as night, and their methods as treacherous as could be devised. No doubt our straightforward Scottishmen are badly armed in their singleness of mind against such snakes that strike them from the dark!"

There was nothing but that curious background of sounds, beyond the stillness. As if an enormous door at an immense distance was standing ajar, and through it one heard the interior echoes of a hall vast as the sky . . .

In the midst of it a particular sound began to stir and come creeping forward till it was half-defined. The faces of the group became overspread with a listening immobility . . . a frowning and straining to locate the increasing sound. Then in the air began a rapid drumming—horses somewhere near at hand had begun to canter. Yet none were in sight! As the incredible forced itself upon them they could only look at each other—those horses were approaching from the south, from behind!

Zzzt—the captain's sword came out of its sheath. The sound was now rising like a wave from the beaten ground. "It *cannot* be!" he muttered, wheeling round. "How could they have passed the scouts?"

There was a flying impression of men getting up by the picket fires, some even running for horses. The group with the captain stood sword in hand with looks sternly resolved—but even yet incredulous—turned on the elbow of the track. Round it a body of horsemen came fast and right upon them.

The surprise was mutual. The newcomers with a number of half-suppressed shouts pulled up sharply and sat peering forward and down, curious and startled. On the other hand the faces of the Menteith men looking up became overspread with fresh amazement as they slowly dropped their points. There was no mistaking those spare muscular forms astride the horses, the high-boned, rugged features and well-spaced eyes . . . Their having passed the scouts unchallenged was no more a mystery. These horsemen were Scots.

Their leader was a tall, narrow man in complete armour. His eyes glinted in the light reflected from his helmet and curving breastplate. In the first surprise he had half-drawn his sword, and he retained his hand on the hilt as he moved his glance from one to another among the faces below, narrowing his eyes in a look at once wary and defiant. At length he smiled—a slow, twisted smile. Slamming the blade back into its sheath he touched the horse and was in motion again, casting as he passed a look from the sides of his narrow eyes.

"What ails yon shamefaced dogs?" said the Menteith captain as the troop swept up to a canter and went past, rising and subsiding in their saddles, with faces held severely to the front or even one might have thought averted. He caught the tall priest's expression as he, too, fixedly regarded the retreating backs, and a look of suspicion came into his frowning face. He swept an alert, awakened glance after the troop, then back at the priest beside him.

"Who *is* yon black-avized man, Reverence? Do you know him?

"I know him . . ." Ninian Kennedy sighed. "That is Pitfourie."

"Pitfourie!" The captain scowled. "What is it I have recently heard about him? Is he not a company-keeper with traitors?"

"So it is said."

The soldier narrowed his eyes on the dark mass retreating, ever more indistinct, undulating, with bobbing heads, along the wood, and his face darkened.

"Traitorous dogs!" he muttered fiercely. "No wonder they were shamefaced. I wonder . . . had they been in the English camp after all? What devil's work have they afoot?"

Ninian Kennedy had also at first looked angry, but his expression had now become, rather, thoughtful and sad. When after a time the soldier spoke again there was a sadness or regretfulness in his tone also . . . "Do you know, Reverence . . . seldom or never have the Englishmen borne the advantage over us except there was division among ourselves." The priest replied only with a slow nodding of his head several times, standing very straight and broad-shouldered, his hands clasped one over the other in front of him. By his side the captain also stood looking after the retreating troop, now one dark roundish mass in front of the trees, that went bobbing and shrinking, while its sound from the hard ground decreased in beats out of time with its throbbing rhythm. But his eyes remained narrowed in suspicion and his face fierce and angry.

They saw the mass at last, grown small, the horses apparently no longer cantering but walking, elongate itself sideways to the right and crawl like a many-legged worm over the line of and into the thick shadows now shrouding the gap through which the English had come not so many hours before, and in which direction now lay the Scottish camp.

They must have been well through the gap, and the two were about to turn away from watching, when from somewhere in the same direction rose in a distant wail the unexpected sound of pipes.

"What is this now?" the captain exclaimed impatiently, thrusting his hands on his hips and glaring.

Another, longer column appeared from a westerly direction, crawling forward. Before touching the line of shadows it began to alter shape: the head seemed to stop while the rest went on marching, until the tail had marched right into the head and there was nothing but one small roundish mass apparently stationary at the end of the wood—but, as was seen in a moment, containing a pulsing movement. In reality the column had inclined upon its right and was advancing along the front of the trees. The roundish mass swelled, the sound of piping grew louder, beating on the air, coming nearer.

The captain called sharply to two men standing near. "To horse and tell those braggart fools to still their clamour! They will bring a herd of the pudding-bellies down on us!"

The two ran to the nearest horses and mounting galloped away along the wood. After a while the pipes came to a wailing stop. A little later the mounted men returned at a canter.

"Men from Cunningham and Kyle," said the first man swinging his leg over the crupper.

The captain whistled. "*Phe-e-ew*! They have had a march!"

"Since yester even at dusk," said the other man dismounting in his turn.

Slowly, under their eyes, the approaching column grew bulkier. The moon far down towards the hills behind, its light flew restlessly and incessantly about in the forest of slanting pikes, coming low enough to show up by and by blue bonnets by the hundred marching in order; but the faces were shadowed, the bodies a long moving blur. Ninian Kennedy was smiling as if to himself; a thoughtful, kindly smile. Somehow, looking at those foot-weary men approaching, he had seemed to himself to hear far, far away the echo of the eager stir of their departure from their homes some more than twelve hours earlier, in the never-ending quarrel of their country.

At a word the whole company halted some score of paces away and their leader came forward—a slim man of middle height, wearing a sword. He gave the impression of being young; although because of the brilliance of the moon his face was shadowed and somewhat indistinct even when he drew up in front of the foremost of the Menteith group, who were the captain and the tall priest standing side by side, their faces clear in bright direct light. Having given each a sharp glance the newcomer raised his right hand to the edge of his bonnet, then placing the hand across his breast made a short bow to each. Speaking in the broad-vowelled Scottish of the south-west he said: "I have the honour to ask you the whereabouts of the enemy!" As he said it he staggered slightly.

The Menteith captain laughed.

"Are you ready for the battle?"

"Ready," replied the newcomer.

The captain laughed even more amusedly . . . "Another of them!"

He turned and pointed with his right hand . . . "The last one of your kind that was here, God rest his foolhardy soul, is lying under that cairn. You want to know where the English are?"—he turned again and pointed with his left in turn—"Just behind that hill. You nearly marched your army straight into their camp, and your pipes squalling."

The other had half-turned to follow the direction, disclosing in the light that fell on his face that he was indeed young, with a young, fair beard. He frowned, seeming to try to grasp the situation.

"The Scots are over yonder," went on the captain, pointing again with his right, "on those heights, and the sooner you get your men there the better, for this is not a position for foot-soldiers. We are only an outpost . . . That is, unless you want to sustain the whole battle on your own account if the English should attack."

When the young man having touched his bonnet turned about to give the necessary orders . . . "Hold!" called the Menteith captain . . . "After all, let them rest here!"—with a laugh—"It will not be for long!"

The other had scarce time to give the orders before his men had reached the ground, some sitting, but most in one movement at their full length.

He turned back to say something. But suddenly swayed towards them. Recovering, he seemed to put up his hand towards the large brooch at his shoulder. But staggered and fell at their feet and began breathing deeply in the snow.

"Here!" called the Menteith captain in a gruff, kindly tone to the two who had done his errand and were standing by. "Wrap the babe in his plaid lest he take a chill!"

The two stooped over him, smiling in their beards. They undid the brooch, rolled him over, then rolling him back wrapped him in the plaid. His eyelids never stirred.

5

The moon with an effect of sudden sinking went down behind the hills, and the silver hours were ended. Darkness everywhere rushed skywards, masses of shadow pouring up from the earth into the deep as if to obliterate the stars, which nevertheless presently were shining out more clearly and brightly. In the new-fallen dark the picket fires floated red, while beyond, away to the north, a dull glow diffused in the heavens marked the Scottish camp and the now dying beacon which had blazed as a guide to parties of men hurrying through the night.

By and by there seemed to come a shifting in the darkness, like its turning on itself. With that a movement of cold air, as if the earth had stirred in its frozen sleep. It might have seemed the stars were paling. Quite suddenly, beyond the darkhung east, an emerald wave of some luminous cold sea tumbled over, and cast a spume of bitter light along the sky. Therewith summits and high snow-covered slopes began gleaming palely all about, creeping from nowhere to hang with a looming presence in the void. Some were to be caught sight of far away, brighter-seeming in their smallness and less mysterious in the recesses of the distance. While this brightness increased in the upper regions and the sky, it appeared for a time to intensify the shadows down below, which lay like a blanket on the levels and thick and impenetrable between the hills. In this lower darkness movement became perceptible and a sound began to rise, and went on swelling: the middle picket fire winked once or twice, then was shouldered continuously out of sight. From the direction of the Scottish camp long lines of cavalry were passing quietly, crossing the burn, continuing southward along the track through the skirts of the wood. After them followed, with a different rhythm, their shapes only just discernible in the diminishing opaque, footmen in innumerable files. All the time overhead the upper layers of the darkness were being touched and made mobile and restlessly evanescent in the constantly descending light, as the surface of a mist is thinned and driven by the wind, and the cold, sheeted hills were rising all around more material and solid. The men of Kyle and Cunningham rose up like a company of ghosts, and were to be distinguished now going down to the burn and into the mouth of the ravine: through the greyness came a series of sharp, splintering sounds from where they were cracking the ice in order to mix with water the handful of oatmeal on which they broke their fast. Reappearing they remounted the bank and stood in order, their forms every instant more solid in the clear-obscure, unmoving; except that—it might have been their pulses passing in so many rhythmic throbs into the shafts which they held upright—above their heads the clearer light, caught on the line of burnished spear-tips like a long filmy scarf entangled, gave forth a certain lambent ripple. All this time the lines of forms were marching across their front, a similar though longer and more marked rhythm of light waving up and down along the spear-points over them. When the last of these had passed the Kyle and Cunningham men moved forward and in a little had gone quietly from the scene.

The company of Menteith men who had been busy with a tightening of girths and overlooking of accoutrements, were now drawn up in readiness: when they mounted, their heads and shoulders rose clear into the growing light. Under that light the features of the frozen face of the world were showing now, rigid and unmysterious.

The captain stopped beside Ninian Kennedy, his arms and armour clear and grey-hard as he sat the great black horse. Inclining in the saddle, his face shadowed under the helmet, the spear-head all the while emitting vicious twinklings high above his head.

"Reverence," he said, low, "we shall not all come out of this . . . Remember our poor souls!"

Their hoof-falls were gone on the frozen ground. Just then the sun rimmed the horizon and swept the whole world in a sudden glory of light no less cold though golden. Ninian Kennedy raised his hand to order the plaid about him. Having earlier given his horse to replace that of a mounted man he set off forward, crossed the burn, and trudged his way on foot along the track between the trees. Among whose wintry branches, stark with the morning, the last tatters of nocturnal shade like belated bats were taking speedy wing.

6

He had not yet won through to the other side when a burst of trumpets rang startlingly out close ahead, with instantly a somewhat emptied postscript in identical notes a distance off. Then he was hearing sounds of shouted commands accompanied by the dry clatter of arms, and hastened his unsure steps on the icy road.

Beyond, in the open, some five thousand of the Scots were drawn up in a line of squares, facing south, their shouldered pikes in a sloping forest leaning towards the wood behind. Apparently they were just on tiptoe of advancing. Out in front were the cavalry, not more than two thousand, drawn out in a thin line which extended the whole length of the spearmen and beyond on either flank. The legs of the horses were being wreathed about, and in a moment had begun to disappear, in an emanation rising from the white ground, so that a minute later they appeared to be treading uneasily in a sea whose surface was breaking belly-high in a froth of swaying foam. Owing to the line of cavalry and the mist together, nothing could be made out of the enemy, although their presence was disclosed by continued urgent trumpetings at no great distance.

As a matter of fact the advantage both of surprise and of position lay at that moment with the Scots. The

English, in the arrogance of their superiority in numbers—which they thought moreover to be greater than it was, since they had not counted on so large a body of Scots reaching the assembly point in a single day and night, especially since beacons were not to have been lighted—and having, as later appeared, reason to suppose that their immunity from defeat was otherwise assured as well; had encamped in a position which placed them now in obvious jeopardy. For a river with steep banks ran transversely across their rear and past the right of their line, and if the advantage went with the Scots in the approaching onset the English could be pushed over the bank into the river. Retreat was impossible. Furthermore the arrival of their outposts to announce the imminent approach of the Scots had found most of them still feasting or about the winecups, in relaxation of fancied security—though no doubt many of the younger and less inured, as well as some perhaps with lingering human feeling, had sought therein to obliterate the sights they continued to see floating before their vision, and dull the sensations they still felt in hand and arm, of defenceless things that not long ago had writhed upon their spears. Altogether they were in meagre heart to face an enemy prepared in sobriety and resolution, burning with resentment and a sense of wrong. Battle however they must accept and that instantly: their opponents were approaching. Throwing forward two or three thousand bowmen as a screen they hastily drew up their line—some footmen in the centre in one solid body and five to six thousand heavily armoured cavalry in two equal divisions on either side.

Among the Scots a peremptory trumpet sounded: the embattled squares moved forward. Mist smoked about their breasts, the helmeted or bonneted heads rising above it, and the masses of tilted pikes glittering and flashing high above in the sharp morning light. The hidden tap and ripple of drums regulated their advance in rigid line with swift steps. In front the horsemen appeared to be swimming their mounts in a foaming sea. They went faster, drawing away ahead, and faster yet, jigged to a trot, lances erect, then at a trumpeted order swept them down to the rest, passing simultaneoutly into a canter. A moment later one horseman here and there among them swayed topheavily, or bowed unaccountably forward and disappeared below the rising surface-level of the mist. One horse standing straight up on its hind legs, with pawing hoofs, was left for a moment an isolated object in the view by the breaking of the rest of the line into a charge which carried them at once out of sight behind the greyish curtain. Indeterminate sounds of shouting came, but whether of men triumphing or being vanquished was impossible to determine, blanketed by the mist.

The squares were continuing their rapid march forward, blindly, in an intensely cold, clammy obscurity that had swallowed them with the rising of the mist above the level of their heads. Almost at once however it was possible to see a little way through it and to make out the squares marching abreast on either side: the sun which appeared to have raised the mist was now summarily dispelling it. A pale effect of blueness began to grow overhead against the sky. Dimly made out forms appeared ahead, which rapidly darkened, and became the Scottish cavalry returning. The drums ceased, trumpets rang out again, and in two—for side and rear ranks three—sharp co-ordinated movements the squares had halted, the sides and rear faced outwards, and the masses of pikes were pointed, motionless and firm, against all airts. The cavalry, having discharged their task of scattering the screen of bowmen, came up and cantered past between the squares towards the rear.

So doing they disclosed the whole English line in movement. Coming out of the mist: the horses' hoofs raising a solid wave of broken snow knee-high, above which their heads strained up and down: on their backs the figures in dull metal sitting, rocking slightly forward and back, their tossing plumes making a rainbow of colour against the even curtain of toneless grey behind, the colours augmented soon by the approaching blazons and devices—all growing implacably taller and solider and swifter in their thunderous on-coming, the snow rolling before them like a billow. The Scots, braced to a rock-like immobility in a deadly silence, waited in their squares, presenting an unflickering wall of points. Against these the English struck with a heavy, splintering crash, and a cry rose and screaming of horses as they were halted and made recoil, while with a ghastly bursting out the colour red sprang to a fluthering predominance over the lines, and the smell of fresh-torn entrails was suddenly as solid as if panted forth by the mass of forms straining and contorting together.

The flanks of the English line, too far extended on either hand, had been bent forward on the impact and left hanging in air. It should have been the task of the Scottish cavalry to charge upon them in that instant of pause while deprived of their momentum—and they were there for the purpose, drawn up in two bodies, one on either flank in the rear of the squares of spearmen, facing outwards. The Menteith captain with his men was near the centre of the body on the left. Looking round to discover why the signal was not given to attack the detached and hesitating portion of the English right, which was before them, and drive it over the river bank behind, he saw nearby a helmet opened, and encountered a mocking glance of two close-set eyes. Eyes which he had seen, unexpectedly coming upon him, late in the previous night. He felt chilled as by a premonition. The moment was passing. The enemy recovered, were reforming their line against them. Still the signal was not given. Presently the sun, which had been showing itself like a great yellow disc whirling in the mist, burst through and sent its cold bright rays flickering straight into the eyes of the Scots. Then the charge was sounded—but among the English. They came forward in a ponderous, straining canter, working up to the gallop, all lances in rest, when at last the bugle among the Scots blew the onset. The Menteith men and another company of about the same number near them with lances pointed sprang impetuously forward in the endeavour to lessen, as much as was still possible, the advantage their opponents now had in both weight of armour and momentum. Then only they perceived they were alone. The great bulk of the Scottish horse, on the sounding of the onset, as at a signal prearranged, had instead of charging wheeled sharply to the left and were now cantering off the field. Thus betrayed to their doom the Menteith men and the others, a hundred against a thousand, charged with a desperate impetuosity. The impact sent many on both sides out of their saddles. The remaining Scots, in the mass of their enemies, made a little agitated swirl which moved forward, slowed down, was surrounded, moved on a little, flickered and died.

On the Scottish right flank the stratagem of the cavalry leaders had gone partially astray. A large proportion of those there, being of a loyalty too notorious, had not been made privy to the traitorous arrangement. These, when they saw that the English opposite them were being allowed to steady themselves and reform, would not wait the signal. Someone among the centre promptly charged and brushed off the end of the English line before them, leaving many mail-clad forms motionless and horses rolling in the snow. The remaining squadrons blew the onset, and the right and half the

Scots, forming the left and left-centre, to the number of about five hundred, carrying out the agreed-on plan, had immediately wheeled right and set to trotting from the field. The English meantime had recovered from their surprise at being attacked, and angered at what they regarded as a piece of treachery, sounded the charge and bore down upon those horsemen trotting so nonchalantly across their front. Thus surprised, a good many of the Scots were emptied from their saddles, a number put spurs to horse and fled the field, but many more, angered at what they considered treachery in turn, or more likely glad to be unbound from the previous treachery, that of their own leaders, set to engaging the enemy and giving hearty thrust for thrust and blow for blow. Meanwhile the loyal five hundred had halted, wheeled about, reformed, and now crashed at full gallop into the English rear, and an extremely fierce, confused, and close-pressed melee ensued upon the spot. This was the moment at which the sun burst through the dissipating mist; and shortly thereafter the English from the other wing, where the horsemen from Menteith and some others had carried out their hopeless charge, began streaming over; whereupon the Scots, now in danger of being overwhelmed with numbers, disengaged themselves wherever they could. Those whose commanders were not traitors, the five hundred, retreated towards some broken, raggedly wooded ground away on the right of the Scottish line; the others drew away northwards, where they were awaited by Pitfourie and a thousand more, sitting their horses observing the progress of things and the effect of their having quit the field.

All this was a diversion. The main engagement was going on between the bulk of the English cavalry—and their foot soldiers, who were now in contact—and the line of Scottish squares. It was being fought on the part of the Scots with extraordinary bitterness. The previous night such as had encountered parties of the English had fought them doggedly, in the spirit of grim familiar work: to-day, incited by the vaunting presence and showy force of the doers of so many outrageous things, every man in the Scottish ranks nourishing an innumerable resentment, fought with a tigerish élan, to which the English could only oppose their sullenness, as it were a weight of resentful phlegm.

The Scottish lines having failed to break, the English after a time sounded the retreat and drew away in order to prepare a second charge. The Scottish spearmen instead of awaiting them, in their impetuosity vaulted over the heaps of dead, and reforming instantly, followed on their heels. This meant the charge had no room to gather impetus and ended ineffectively, with a loud clattering and the immediate fall of a number of knights, against the spears. The lines however were again engaged down their whole length, with extreme noise and clangour. To the eye they resembled a band of burnished black, variegated with colours and scintillatings, drawn across the snow which the sun, unimpeded now by any shreds of mist, was causing to glitter everywhere —except on the ground of the first engagement, where there were heaps over which red nets appeared to have been thrown, rendering them uniformly dull, and which were giving forth a kind of slow smoke, or steam. Past these smoking heaps came at speed the English who had been engaged with the Scottish cavalry, to attack the squares from the rear, and the contest was fully joined with great energy on every side.

But with the same lack of effect. In spite of repeated charges the wall of pikes could not be breached. Moreover the horsemen were losing heavily, their casualties impeding them more and more. When a spearman fell his place was instantly taken by the man behind: while the bowmen shooting from within the squares did fearful execution; against cavalry held at pike point every bolt or arrow finding its mark in horse or man. In the centre the two bodies of foot, Scots and English, had been locked weapon to weapon, like fighting bulls, in an immobility that belied the violent energy being put forth on either side. But the English foot, who were not of the same quality as their cavalry, showed signs of giving ground. Their doing so would have meant the elimination of the entire right wing of English horse, whom the Scottish squares in centre and left wing by swinging round could have enclosed and pressed over the river bank. The danger was obvious: the cavalry of the right wing abruptly discontinued the attack and wheeled away to extricate themselves. At that very moment a large part of the centre gave way, the footmen in fleeing came right in the path of their own cavalry and numbers of their running forms could be seen going down like stuffed men under the horses' surging breasts. The whole English centre and right were thus in loose motion and the corresponding area of the Scottish line pressing forward with cries of "On them! On them!"—while the Scottish right were still held immobile by masses of English cavalry pushing the attack upon it in front, in rear, and on the further flank. Its squares were holding firm—the flags of some burghs were seen standing up steadily like the masts of stranded ships amongst the surf. They must have been glad nonetheless of the partial distractions afforded by the loyal five hundred Scottish horsemen, who had been emerging in a series of sorties from the broken, wooded area in which they had sought shelter and attacking the English from the rear.

The advance of the left and centre had bent the Scottish line forward at an angle; the left now actually resting on the river bank. In front of them the ground was clearing of English, both foot and horse, but for the jetsam of dark, trampled forms scattered here and there. The Scots standing in the squares had at last a respite in which to breathe deeply and freely of the cold air, to wipe their brows, bind up wounds, and stretch their necks to the right to see how it went with their comrades there, whose position could be deduced from the great press of horsemen about them thrusting and smiting at something in their midst, and also by the occasional glimpse of one of their standards disclosed by a movement of the crowded figures. They would then cast their glances up into the clear shallow sky, at the sun not greatly risen above the horizon though already well on its journey across the south, lighting the up-raised cheeks and eyes of those in the front ranks of the squares. The opposite bank of the river was not thirty yards distant from the square farthest to the left. A well-grown wood of hazel clothed its sloping side. Out of the tree tops shot a flock of little birds, out of the wood into the sun, and away down the sky, a swarm of dots at one moment, almost invisible, the next a shower of brazen particles as they swerved like one thing and caught the sun on all the little wings, till at last with a long, steady, sailing descent they checked, flew apart like corn out of a fist, and dropped from sight into another wood dark in the middle distance. The eyes of many men in the squares had followed them in their free flight.

Now that the enemy had all cleared away in front, the voice of the river—a hoarse and profound note—was audible side by side with the noise of the combat on the wing. Then it could be heard that the river had a second voice also, running on above the sullen rumble —an icy hiss. These two voices sounding together continuously had a note in common, hostile, minatory and implacable. Except that ever and anon a deep, hollow, pealing tone, a music of rocky underwater chasms, welled up through the heavier voice and sounded out a moment liquid and many-harmonied, when also the hissing voice would break for an instant into iridescent tinklings, before both dropped again to rancour, gnawing and chill.

But something was afoot. Among the English they were sounding the retreat. Those engaged with the right of the Scots broke off and went trailing away across the trampled plain; creating a duller impression as they went than when they had first appeared all burnished in the morning. The squares of the right wing were thus disclosed again to view, standing where they had been standing all along behind that screen and press of cavalry. Their fronts noticeably dulled with blood. For some minutes after their opponents had withdrawn to a distance they remained rigid, almost as if inanimate. Then though no man stirred a hairsbreadth from his place life and movement broke out again among them, like a wave passing through the ranks. In a long, slow ripple the bloodied pike heads began rising, reached the perpendicular. The men in the ranks looked about them, with a kind of surprise on seeing again the familiar vista of the white world—a surprise tinged to solemnity, and caused, indeed, by an image still persisting before their wearied senses, of the dancing, kaleidoscopic huddle in front of their spears: an impression of a perpetually tumbling wave filled with horses' teeth and blood-shot nostrils, ears wickedly laid back and straining, sidelong eyes, hoofs rising up and plunging straight down, interspersed with devices on surcoats, and gleaming head-pieces, metal men in their saddles lifting their metal arms; all pressing continuously with an inhuman weight, till eye and hand were deadened and another man within one took command and held the shaft like rock endlessly beyond the holding point. The bearded faces in the front ranks were turned, looking with the same suggestion of stern interest, if not surprise, at the lines of their comrades in the centre squares, and the others farther off, right away to the extreme left standing above the river; and all these in turn looked sternly back, as at those they might never have expected to see again, or whose ordeal, reinforcing the recent recollection of their own, made a solid inward sense of sharp heights of experience surmounted together, if not also still to be traversed with effort even to agony.

For it was never supposed that the English had withdrawn finally. Everyone in fact turned to looking out from the squares, sweeping the ground with their eyes for indications of the tactic in composition. The English had formed in line extending in front of the right wing of the Scots, round their flank and some way along their rear. When they left-turned they formed a column, which then moved forward, its head passing down along the rear of the Scots towards their left wing, while its tail was moving along the front of the Scottish right and round its flank. They went at the slow, walking pace of their horses. Some plumes still made a brave display, with their colours bright against the distant snow-slopes, but many were dishevelled and drooping. The backwards and forwards motion of a man in armour on a moving horse was exaggerated in some cases to a hinted top-heaviness. One man-at-arms on a flecked brown horse turned aside out of the moving column not far along the rear of the squares, and actually came riding slowly toward the Scottish lines; but after a few paces halted. His action had drawn the enquiring notice of a great many of the Scots: those of his own side also as they rode past behind him were turning their heads. He was simply sitting there, with an air of brooding. Those nearest him could now see that the whole of the horse's fore-parts and flanks were being darkly stained. The man changed his brooding air for what appeared to be a great interest in the ground in front of his horse's feet. An intense interest, since it seemed to draw him farther and farther down and forward. As abruptly however he seemed to abandon it for the idea of going to sleep, appearing to try to rest his cheek against the horse's neck. At the same moment he discarded his lance, which fell to the ground. Meanwhile the foremost of the English had touched the river bank, the whole column halted and faced inwards in a continuous line from end to end in rear of the Scottish squares and round their right flank. The solitary horseman was a conspicuous figure between the two armies: many eyes under iron cowls or through metal slits were regarding him with as narrow an attention as if the fortune of the day hung upon his movements. Thus invested with a nimbus of significance the apparently drowsy horseman gave a portentous nod, and tumbled straight down from the saddle. In the hush that hung about the field the impact of his armoured form upon the armoured ground was distinctly heard, muffled only by the carpet of snow. His foot remained caught in the stirrup, the horse continuing to stand motionless. One of his own side rode forward and tried to disengage the foot from the stirrup with a twist of his inserted lance-point, and failing approached and bending over did it with his hand, and with a tap of his lance set the horse trotting riderless away. After looking down at the prostrate man from the saddle he left him and returned as he had come and wheeling his horse about backed into his place in the line and at once became indistinguishable.

The dead or dying man's horse, as it went, trailed away with it as it were the curtain of curious interest that had for a little clouded the purpose of their being there, and confronted them again with each other's hostility. The question was the plan or purpose the English had in mind, and it was not answered by their having drawn up in line of attack—for the men they were now facing, in the rear of the squares, were the freshest in the field, having, with the exception of those on the right wing, had little to do all the day: and furthermore in their present position the English were disadvantaged by having the sun, standing in the south, striking full in their faces or flickering through the slits in their visors. To attack from this new position tormed therefore at the most only a part of their plan, as the Scots were well aware even while their left with a wary shuffling movement and with lowered pikes drew back somewhat nearer the English and their right at the same time moved forward away from them and so straightened their line. The enemy made no attempt to interfere with these movements, merely retracting their own left and advancing their right so as to be still parallel with their opponents.

Now the plan was no longer uncertain. A half-shout that was also a kind of groan from the Scots front ranks marked its disclosure . . . *Bowmen*!

These after being scattered at the beginning of the engagement by the charge of the Scottish cavalry through the mist, had sought safety behind their own lines. Now they were seen farther up the river, having emerged from their place of refuge where they had been reassembled. At the sight of them coming running forward, a stooping crowd of figures fitting their arrows to their bowstrings as they ran, and the numbers of them blackening the snow, the shout that was also like a groan went up among the squares and there were bitter maledictions on the traitor gentry who had deserted with the horse, thus depriving the footmen of the only effective counter to this species of attack. Almost all the Scottish bowmen had ere now become replacements in the ranks of pikemen, but even if still supplied with ammunition they could have been of small avail against such numbers.

The part of the English cavalry was now clear; they were to remain just out of bowshot, too close for the spearmen to risk any rapid evading movement, until the archers at their leisure had thinned out their ranks, when the cavalry would sweep away the remnants in one triumphant charge. Already they visibly animated themselves in prospect of action, a sinister gleam from their arms breaking all down the line.

The bowmen came in to nigh a hundred paces and loosed off a flight which passed like a swift shadow through the air and alighting barbed the ground before the pikemen and caused a movement like a tremor among the men in the front ranks as one here and there fell against his neighbour or sank to earth. Simultaneously however an urgency of trumpets had broken out among the squares, and a second lethal covey had not quit the wood of lifted bows before the whole line was in motion leftwards; and it had not alighted, causing the same tremor in the ranks, before the square on the extreme left had dropped out of sight over the river bank and its place been taken by the next in order. As the cavalry were close in, constantly feinting as if to charge, the movement had to be carried out with lowered pikes along the rear ranks, slowly, those heart-breaking discharges coming over with a hiss more venomous than that of the river, followed always by the same choked-down cries and men tumbling among their fellows.

For the front ranks a momentarily unlifting sight was

the remaining Scottish cavalry, looking few though all the more intrepid in the sweep of white landscape, stretching out from their wooded and broken cover away to the right, in a determined attempt to reach the bowmen and throw confusion in their ranks. They could not possibly have succeeded, however: from the English right wing a much heavier body of horse detached themselves, leaving the spearmen for the present, and went hammering away to intercept them; and some kind of hand-to-hand engagement was seen to be in progress at a considerable distance from the archers. The deadly showers therefore continued to deplete the ranks, and the squares notwithstanding to move with a steady, regular motion leftwards. Two more of them in succession reached the brink and breaking up into their component individuals disappeared over into temporary safety: then the section of cavalry nearest to the river charged the square presently a-top the bank. Their object was by pinning down those nearest the bank to hold up the entire line, on the rest of which the archers might continue to shower their deadly shafts. But only those squares halted which were actually attacked, the rest by inclining forward could pass behind them, and the leftwards movement continued. They were able to move but slowly, however, despite the terrible anxiety to quit the spot, because of the enemy hanging close in and threatening every moment to come down on them. So step by step the wall of spears grew thinner; as they moved they left a trail of men scattered on the ground.

A wind sprang up in the clear north-east, blowing strongly through the empty heavens: those down below on earth felt its movement. Felt it flutter and sway. With a sustained, long hollow pipe or hoot wavering away into the south-west the wind steadied and in one mass the whole space of air moved forward solidly. At that the snow floor stirred and lifted. Its surface was weaved over by broad, fluthering lines. Where two or three of these met in their darting courses the winnowed snow flew up in a powdery column. Behind such a column a section of the bowmen, or a group of the horsemen fighting at a distance, would suddenly become grey and indistinct, even for a moment invisible; and then immediately dark and solid and in place again as the tower as quickly toppled or collapsed from sight, or became a madly contorting spiral that rushed vanishing away.

Above the line of the river bank the heads of pikes could be seen moving along in procession: those who had disengaged themselves were making their way upstream to a ford some fifty paces distant. Linked together, they were crossing this thigh deep in rapid water, and climbing up among the tree trunks on the further bank. In this way more than half had crossed or were crossing when from the bank where the remainder were still combatant desperate cries and exultant shouts went up. The bowmen had ceased upon a signal to send their arrows over, and the right wing, the most exhausted in the earlier part of the battle and the most depleted by the arrows, were attacked front, rear and further flank by the full weight of cavalry and were in danger of breaking. "Back! back!" sharply echoed the cries among the trees: the cries in the river—"Back! back!"—were liquified and carried away downwards, becoming hoarsened in the moment of mingling with the note of the water. All turned about and began pressing back across the river.

The cries among the clashing forms on the opposite bank grew ever more desperate, ever more exultant. The small red-haired priest was standing among the leafless trees on the wooded further bank, his face blue, and drawn with the agony of fatigue, shivering in violent spasms inside drenched clothes turning to ice as high as his waist: his eyes held on the imminent disaster. A man passing overheard his involuntary exclamation. He stopped.

"What's that, Maister Erskine?"—he shouted above the noise of the conflict and the river—"Aye, ye speak truth . . . a bloody beast the Southron!"

The face the man had turned was startling, the shouting mouth a kind of dark cavern in moustaches and beard of solid white ice from the freezing of the breath he had but now been panting forth in the extremity of exertion, his eyes, deep-sunken in his head, burning with the fever of fatigue under twin ice-curtains of eyebrows . . .

The shouts rising still louder on the other bank he recollected himself and turning his ice-encumbered face went off quickly, managing his pike among the trees.

Not far away Ninian Kennedy was standing, his hands pressed together while his lips moved soundlessly; his eyes fixed on those thin lines of spears on the other bank which could be seen through the trellis of branches, as if to work a miracle by their intensity.

A solid splashing was rising from the river as they crossed in a manful column linked together. Then the splashing suddenly dropped away and down there also shouting started, and among the crowd waiting to enter. There was a second of only the river's voice, then the shouts recommenced, and the splashing in a less solid way, suggesting agitation or disorderly haste. Arrows had begun falling among them. Bowmen had appeared thick on the bank upstream. Now it seemed that all was over: the right were held and being slowly pounded by the English cavalry, the left and centre could not reach them for the arrows in the ford.

But as suddenly the arrows ceased. It was the archers' turn to break out into crying and shouting. Beyond them had risen up a cloud of snow, and against its grey mass the bowmen were seen as dark forms leaping this way and that, all their heads rigidly turned in the direction *away* from the river and the men in it. Strange noises like animal roaring came intermingled with their shouts, and all at once large shapes—non-human shapes—were seen, cloudily, plunging about among their darting forms in a denser cloud of snow, and louder cries were rising. It was the resource of the indefatigable remnant of

Scottish cavalry that had been equal after all to stopping that fatal archery. Frustrated in their attempt to reach the bowmen across the open they had made a wide detour and re-approached unseen from the south-west. Rushing the English camp they had thrown down some stockades penning stolen cattle and stampeded them in the direction of the river, following them right in among the bowmen, who were instantly converted into a panic-stricken mob.

The spearmen in the ford were quick to avail themselves of their immunity. The iron line was again uncoiling from the trees and measuring the breadth of the river with surging tread, pikes bristling above. But their pace increased still more, with a sudden, forward impulse, when changed cries from the bank told of a break in the tension of things and a falling of fortune against their own side. The square on the extreme right, the most borne upon all the day, had in fact at last presented too thin a line of spears against the horses' armoured breasts. These had burst their way inside at first one then several points, and that cry of the English had gone up that meant "the kill." A single moment and they were in the centre of the square, and it was broken up into isolated, still resisting fragments. The flag, which had remained erect all day, rocked about as if shaken by a tempest: fell, appeared once again over the heads of the smiting and exulting horsemen, then sank forever. The groups were soon reduced. Any horrified eye in the squares that remained intact could have caught sight only of isolated pikemen still erect in the melee, and those, cloaked in their own life's blood, making some last blind staggering lunges while their enemies struck them at their will until they kneed the ground and fell their length, and perhaps knew for a little the flowing out of their life and the lessening smart of indifferent hoofs spurning their clay.

The spearmen out of the river were running to place their shafts together, and the enemy, not to be caught between two walls of points, broke off their somewhat flagging efforts and retired at a wearied canter, which promptly became a walk. Their seated backs were seen in long lines above drooping tails which the wind bent away sideways. Over their helmeted heads the pennons though heavy with blood snapped like scorpions in the crying wind, even at moments stood straight out from the rippling lance-shafts in their upright rows. The snow smoking from every hoof.

The spearmen threw forward a semi-circle of the fresher men of the left-wing who had returned across the river and behind these the fragments of the depleted right made their best haste from the field and down the bank. But although the English halted, wheeled, reformed, and even came some way forward—the bright, low sun evoked few sparklings on their armour now—they contented themselves with hanging menacingly close in, giving those on the bank no occasion but to retire below it as soon as that could in orderly wise be done.

In the shouting ford they were still contending against troubles. Only four or five could cross abreast; moreover they were hampered by wounded men who were being assisted or carried forward: worse, a number of bowmen had restationed themselves on the bank above. To increase confusion some hundred horsemen arrived upon the scene. All that remained of the loyal five hundred of the right wing, they appeared from nowhere, covered with blood. In their midst was the Bishop. His helmet dented, his face like chalk, his eyes filmed and unseeing, he was all but lying on the horse's neck, while from the point of his sword, which still hung from his hand, his blood dripped slowly down. In this state he was led across, followed by his grey-faced, blood-splashed crew conspicuous at straggling intervals amongst the pikemen who themselves were no less hollow-eyed, and might by their appearance, some of them, have been wallowing over head in blood.

Of five thousand spears that had begun the day scarce four were making the passage through the river. Every now and then one, either pierced by an arrow or weakened by his wounds, fell, slipped from his comrades' frozen clutch and was instantly swept from sight into deep water. The others went on. The cloud-mass that unnoticed had been racing down the whole sky lipped across the sun and there fell everywhere a greyness, and with it a feeling of more cold. Like capfuls of white feathers snowflakes came to meet them down the shrilling wind. Through the malevolent voice of the river, deep and hoarse, their splashing rose with urgent iciness . . . At last their hasty legs were brushing the snow in ferny hollows of the wood.

After them came the voice of the abandoned field. Many of them, recalling the dishonoured cause of their misfortunes, stood still in the falling snow.

* * *

But the field heard later and other voices. Voices of gruff command, clinkings of arms, hoof-beats and footfalls, all the opaque grey-pallid snow-filled night . . . following, ever-following south. Christ in the will, the blow befallen earlier was nothing . . . not even a feather.